CW00802761

TWISTED TALES

2022

A TALE HIDDEN

Edited By Byron Tobolik

First published in Great Britain in 2022 by:

Young Writers
Remus House
Coltsfoot Drive
Peterborough
PE2 9BF
Telephone: 01733 890066
Website: www.youngwriters.co.uk

All Rights Reserved
Book Design by Ashley Janson
© Copyright Contributors 2022
Softback ISBN 978-1-80459-225-0

Printed and bound in the UK by BookPrintingUK
Website: www.bookprintinguk.com
YB0523U

FOREWORD

Welcome, Reader!

Are you ready to step into someone else's shoes and experience a new point of view?

For our latest competition *Twisted Tales*, we challenged secondary school students to write a story in just 100 words that shows us another side to the story. They could add a twist to an existing tale, show us a new perspective or simply write an original tale. They were given optional story starters and plot ideas for a spark of inspiration, and encouraged to consider the impact of narrative voice and theme.

The authors in this anthology have given us some unique new insights into tales we thought we knew, and written stories that are sure to surprise! The result is a thrilling and absorbing collection of stories written in a variety of styles, and it's a testament to the creativity of these young authors.

Here at Young Writers it's our aim to inspire the next generation and instill in them a love of creative writing, and what better way than to see their work in print? The imagination and skill within these pages are proof that we might just be achieving that aim! Congratulations to each of these fantastic authors.

CONTENTS

Shirebrook Academy, Shirebrook

Isabel Vale (14)	56
Bentley Mohammed (14)	57
Maja Fidali (14)	58
Sophie Ball (14)	59
Demi-Leigh Harvey (14)	60
Jennifer McIntyre (14)	61
Harrison Robson (14)	62
Axel Steers (12)	63
Ella Murcott (14)	64
Braydon Johnson (12)	65
Kornelia Kandyba (13)	66
Joshua Lewin (14)	67
Alexa Baker (13)	68
Gabriel Rodgers (12)	69
Kacie Boulton (13)	70
Enoch Donkor (13)	71
Roxy Key (11)	72
Hope Sykes (13)	73
Owen Thorpe (14)	74
Oliver Hough (14)	75
Lillie Mower (13)	76
Lucy Williams (12)	77
Logan Middleton (14)	78
Abigail Holmes (14)	79
Joshua Kirk (14)	80
Ciara Wormall (12)	81
Harley Buckingham (13)	82
Kaitlyn Hutchinson-Price (12)	83
Ava Shaw (14)	84
Tilly Starkey (13)	85
Jessica Shipman (14)	86
Lillie Hunt (14)	87
Teigan Gascoigne (14)	88
Lucas Thomas (14)	89
Faye Newton (14)	90
Isabelle Tipple	91
Tyler Buxton (14)	92
Brandon Sherwood (14)	93
Carter Laker (13)	94
Milly Merrington (13)	95

The Highcrest Academy, High Wycombe

Sophie Smith (14)	96
Naomi Lyon	97
Saarah Mahmood (14)	98
Gemma Eames	99
Leah Mills	100

Wellington School, Timperley

Oscar Field (12)	101
Ryan Pickup	102
Arthur Finney (14)	103
James Barnes (12)	104
Amy Fielding (13)	105
Mason Onyemem (13)	106
Sufyaan Farid (14)	107
Alice Stephens (13)	108
Elijah Lyttle (13)	109
Joe Tan (12)	110
Neve Henderson (14)	111
Joseph Turner (13)	112
Isabelle Taylor (13)	113
Zak Adams (13)	114
Benjamin Mudd (13)	115
Lola Brumby (13)	116
Daniel Lamb (13)	117
Emaan Humayun (14)	118
Jacob Cleevely (12)	119
Seiji Ivison (13)	120
Thomas Weilding (14)	121
Calico Kee (13)	122
Isabelle-Louise Salinger (13)	123
Amelie Greaves (12)	124
George Wood (12)	125
Alex Senior (13)	126
Abigail Turl (14)	127
Emma Donohue (14)	128
Nathan Collinge (13)	129
Rosie Brown (13)	130
Megan Laffly (14)	131
Jasmine-Katie Orpet (14)	132
George Albinson-Myers (13)	133

THE
STORIES

WOLFY VS THE THREE LITTLE PIGS

Wolfy was tending crops on his eco farm when the growl of bulldozers shattered the peace. Three pig-shaped shadows loomed over the hill.

"Get off my land!" Wolfy shouted, wielding his trusty shovel and advancing towards the action. Shells of houses were being constructed on his organic cornfield.

Huffing and puffing, he attempted to blow the houses down. Squealing, laughing pigs fueled his anger. They refused to move. Wolfy stressed about how to save his farm.

Over tea, he told his family about the goings-on. "So that's what happens when you don't respect the environment... More pork stew anyone?"

Lars Hunter (11)
Allerton Grange School, Leeds

HARRY POTTER: THE DEATHLY HALLOWS FINAL FIGHT

Harry can't believe his eyes. Hogwarts is on fire. Voldemort and his warriors have begun conquering the good side. The army of Harry Potter begins to disintegrate fast as the only remaining survivors are Harry, Ron and Hermione. As Voldemort takes his final strike at the castle, *crash!* The towering, magical school collapses with Ron getting crushed to death instantly. Harry and Hermione scatter away from death until they lose each other. "Help!" A sound beneath the rocks breaks the silence all around Harry. Harry's traumatised, unable to run anywhere and struck with an Avada Kedavra as Voldemort triumphs.

Nicholas Kironji (12)
Allerton Grange School, Leeds

PANDORA'S BOX

I had a dream about 'the box'. Again. It was calling me.
Unlike before, I witnessed my world deprived of love, for
hatred was unknown. Nor did they feel joy, for sorrow was a
stranger. Friendship was non-existent.
At that pivotal moment, I awoke, and my fingers hesitantly
lifted the gilded lid, and to my despair, out flew all evils... yet
a glowing flicker of *'elips'* - hope.
I'd seen a world void of hope - and without hope, there was
nothing - no wisdom, courage, moderation or justice; no
chances were taken to achieve those virtues.
Until curiosity unleashed hope.

Sumayyah Begum (15)
Allerton Grange School, Leeds

THE NEW QUEEN

We feared the Red Queen. Everyone did, but us flamingos, most of all. The sickening crunch of beak against quills, the clammy hands gripping our ankles with painful abandon, the realisation that we could do nothing being the most chilling. The first queen was lenient, amused by our indignant squawks, our craning necks that offset the newcomers. The second considered our flailing to be disobedience, adjusting our necks with increasing anger before snapping one. So, when the royal fanfare blew, the chant slipped off our tongues like honey, thick with deceit and terror.

"All hail, Alice, the Queen of Hearts."

Maya Manota (15)
Allerton Grange School, Leeds

HUNT FOR CINDERELLA

I inspected the evidence in front of me: a grainy CCTV photograph, two eyewitness reports, and a glass slipper. Sirens wailed in the distance. How were we going to find this woman? In the photo, she wore an enormous silver dress, as if from a fairy tale, and was entering a distinctively pumpkin-orange car. Prince Charming approached me and my team earlier that night, asking us to track down this woman, supposedly called 'Cinderella'. Now police cars were racing around the city - a full-scale manhunt. Her crime? Theft of thousands of pounds worth of jewellery from the prince's ball.

Oliver Johns (14)
Allerton Grange School, Leeds

THE HIDDEN TRUTH

I'm Elise, you may know me as the 'evil queen'. Snow White's truly evil. *She* murdered her father and attempted to get rid of me. I realised, but it was too late. I was well known for my complexion, before those vile potions Snow White concocted made me hideous. She spread malicious rumours, then fled, knowing I'd be framed for her death. I made those lies the truth... Poisoned her like she poisoned me! Until that prince saved her. Suddenly, I became the evil queen. I wish for justice but Earth's too corrupt to understand. My life remains a mystery...

Nirmala Paul (12)
Allerton Grange School, Leeds

MIDAS

My fingernails reflected the sunlight streaming through the grand arched windows. Olive skin turned golden by my father's caress. I stared impassively as he collapsed at my feet, running his hands over the cold, shiny ripples of my robe in wordless horror. He'd chased the warm glow gold promised for many years, yet had only just learned how achingly immovable it truly was. My smile was the soft, laughing beam of a loving son, but now it glittered. I fit into his beautiful shiny world among platters of gilded fruits, cups, and diadems. I was his perfectly golden boy.

Sophie Leach (15)
Allerton Grange School, Leeds

REWRITE HISTORY: WWII, IF THE NAZIS HAD WON

When the Russian troops marched into Germany, Hitler wiped out all the allies. He'd blown all of the allies' military bases to dust. The Nazis had won. In England, you could smell the burning of all the bodies. In every neighbourhood, you could see shattered windows and broken doors. I saw the schools for the Aryan race, they were taught how every Jew was bad and how the Nazis were always right. The school was centred around a park where the sign: *'Heil Hitler'* was, and in the far corner, I could see several statues of the Nazi party.

Rafiza Khatun (14)
Allerton Grange School, Leeds

I REMEMBER

I remember. I remember waking up violently in a room I did not recognise, asking myself: *Who am I? Where am I? Why? Why?* I remember the chains. The chains surrounding me, ensnaring me like an insect in a spider's web. I remember the days shrieking at the cobbled walls, deeply wishing for something to happen, to change, even though deep down I knew it wouldn't be answered.

No longer. No longer will I be trapped. No longer will I stay vulnerable. I will break free from these chains. I will be free. I will rise.

Leonardo Salvarani (14)
Allerton Grange School, Leeds

NEVER A SECOND CHANCE

Everything is a horrendous disaster. Edmund's stubbornness has caused us to be here. Now that Aslan's gone, we're never going to win this. Lucy and Susan have gone to help find Aslan. The deceitful White Witch made sure to manoeuvre us. Thoughts race through me as I try to hastily think about the time that I have to save us all. I, Peter, am going to save us. But as I look across the field, there is a scream, then a thud. The White Witch towers over us, pale as snow, turning the whole landscape to ice... freezing us all.

Ana Kironji (13)
Allerton Grange School, Leeds

WAITING FOR RED

Pain shot through my head as I lay there barely able to breathe because of the illness I had. I hoped that my granddaughter would be here soon. A sudden creak at the door. I lifted my head, delighted at my granddaughter's presence, except it wasn't her. I gasped at the sight of a huge wolf grinning mischievously at my weak state. I didn't even get a chance to scream. He licked his lips and towered over me, his smile growing wider. He opened his mouth full of teeth. I closed my eyes and they didn't open again.

Zayd Bashir (14)
Allerton Grange School, Leeds

HUMPTY DUMPTY

It was a normal day until Humpty Dumpty fell off a wall. He was picked up by an ambulance. The doctors fixed him easily, to his relief. He was shown the amount he had to pay, but Humpty Dumpty didn't have enough money. The doctors weren't pleased and gave him the opposite of treatment. They put him on a wall again and pushed him over. However, this wasn't the first time they pushed Humpty Dumpty. In fact, they did it to start with. They did it to take his money. They had run this scam many times, but got nothing.

Alfie Whitehead (14)
Allerton Grange School, Leeds

VILLAIN

Nobody knows the truth about me. They all think that I'm the evil one. But in reality, the so-called heroes are ruining the world. Villains live in the old rundown houses trying to protect humanity, but the heroes live in the big mansions with private rooms where they plot their evil plan to eliminate all the villains and to manipulate our people into feeding into their plan to control the world. Every night, I go to bed and wake up drenched in sweat because there is no AC in my house because I can't afford it.

Evren Odabas (14)
Allerton Grange School, Leeds

THE FARMER'S BRIDE

From the farmer's perspective

Nobody knows the truth about me. They are all convinced she is just another innocent woman. I try to tell them but they won't listen to me. I have managed to escape a few times but she always catches me and traps me once again. Is this all because I'm a man?

Every morning, I wake up to the same abuse, the same control and the same old nasty woman I know her to be. This evening, I managed to escape to the loft and she still hasn't found me yet until the sound of creaking stairs suddenly awakens me...

Hannah Back

Allerton Grange School, Leeds

THE TRUTH BEHIND MY FAIRY TALE

I have never needed saving. The fact is, I actually like my life, even though everyone thinks it's miserable. I have gone through some pretty messed up stuff. I know I'm an orphan. Losing my parents made me realise that life sucks. Deal with it. As for my stepmother, she seems evil, but she's just as broken as the rest of us. So when this alleged Prince came into my life, I was like, *No, thank you*. Long story short, I lost my shoe and he fell in love with me. Such a pathetic way to fall in love.

Sofia Din (13)
Allerton Grange School, Leeds

JOKER'S BACKSTORY

Why did the Joker become a villain?

When I was young, only 13 years old, I got bullied and beaten up at school. I was what people nowadays call a 'nerd', which I got sick of. I ended up planning the murder of a student, a student who tried to hit me. So I dragged him outside and beat him up. Everyone thought I was a villain, but I was only defending myself...

The Joker told so many different stories about his life, he had no true identity. He kept a lot of stuff about his life to himself.

Kaden Lopez (14)
Allerton Grange School, Leeds

FROM THE KING'S VIEW (AFTER EVER AFTER)

Even now while I write this, I still am only able to barely recollect what I had seen in Dutton's apartment that night. The unfathomable beauty of it all. I can swear up to the heavens that what I saw was beauty imagined by beings we can only scratch to understand. It was all written there on that divine tome wrapped in sickly, yellow skin. A promise; made to me. My own kingdom, my dear queen and great riches. It promised me all of that and more. I hereby renounce all I knew. All hail the Debauched King.

Mikhail Lukach (18)
Allerton Grange School, Leeds

THE RED APPLE

Magically, an apple was sat there on the window. I picked up the apple, admiring its colour and perfection. Although I wanted to take a big juicy bite, I thought it would make the perfect snack for all my seven friends. I cut the apple into seven equal pieces and placed them all on separate plates. Shortly after, they all came home and took a big bite out of all their apple pieces. Moments later, I heard a simultaneous thud and ran to the front room to see all my dwarf friends flat out on the floor.

Melissa Greenberg (12)
Allerton Grange School, Leeds

PETER'S POV

I was in the bar drinking. My mate went out for a smoke; everyone was quite drunk. I felt nauseous as I got shoved towards the edge of the table, stomach-first. She came up to me: pretty. She asked me to follow her. I did. I obeyed her like a lamb heading to slaughter by its owner. It was a motel room. We stepped in but something felt really unsettling. Hair at the back of my neck stood up but I ignored it. She came in for a kiss - colder than pewter. My vision went blurry. I saw her smirk...

Aisha Arifeen (14)
Allerton Grange School, Leeds

THE CHANGE

When I was 12, life was going well until one day, my dad started getting more and more ill. Then one day, he sadly passed. Since then, life hasn't been so normal - none of my friends knew until they asked me why I was sad, so I told them. Now, they are much more aware. I had to get counselling but that didn't help at all. Also, I don't like a specific date every month, so writing about my feelings takes a little weight off my shoulders and sometimes it makes me a lot happier.

Jess Beer (13)
Allerton Grange School, Leeds

THE PARTY

'Twas gloomy and late at night. The party would commence in 20 minutes - my friend was giving me a lift.
Adam soon pulled up in the driveway as I was biding my time on the porch. I got in the car at nine twenty-eight. The party started at ten to, he couldn't wait. I felt thumping on my back the whole way, with the heating and radio on full blast. *How peculiar*, I thought. We parked at Archer's Close, locked the car and left for the house. They asked me where Scott and Alan were. "Enjoying the heating," I remarked.

Harvey Bassnett (13)
Cardinal Heenan Catholic High School, West Derby

THE WOODS

I wanted to be a movie producer when I grew up. It was my dream. One day, we got given the task of making a short film. Luckily, my friend, Ron, also took classes with me, so I thought we could work together. We chose to venture out into the woods so our short film would stand out.

We packed our bags and got our 'equipment', it was really just water and our phones. We went deep into the forest, but my friend just suddenly stood there. When I turned around, I was somewhere else. Then I saw something...

Oliver Turek (13)
Cardinal Heenan Catholic High School, West Derby

LITTLE RED RIDING HOOD

No one knows the truth about me. I am always made out to be the bad guy in tales, but let me tell you what really happened...

I was trying to guide her through the treacherous forest full of nasty surprises. When I saw her granny leave the house, I immediately rushed inside; simply because I did not want her to travel such a long way for nothing. I tried to roleplay as her granny. However, the moment she realised, she screamed and sprinted directly out. I then fled the forest, never to be seen again.

George Parry (12)
Cardinal Heenan Catholic High School, West Derby

MACBETH

I was slowly trudging down the hallway peering through every oak door looking for number 35. Two guards were sleeping outside his room, ankle to neck in silver armour with decently-sized lances in both hands. I opened the door, knife in hand, grinning at how easy this deed was. It was too perfect, no guards, everyone asleep, just me and the king. I hung my hand up high and struck the king. I knew my coronation was tomorrow. I left the bloody knife in the hand of the guard. Macbeth was king.

George Bowers (12)

Cardinal Heenan Catholic High School, West Derby

THE QUIET EARTH

I was driving through the countryside, it was five miles to the next town. It was quiet out there. I just thought it was nothing until I got to the town of Ark Ville. Everyone was just standing still, no one was moving. I thought it might have been a hoax or something, but I went over to one of the civilians and they weren't even breathing. But then I saw someone moving. He was dressed in all black like a demon and then he saw me. I ran, but he was faster than me and then...

Alfie Goodwin (13)

Cardinal Heenan Catholic High School, West Derby

VIKING RAID

"We shall go on a raid!" I shouted. My warriors raised their horns of mead. The next day, we ran across the grassy land for hours until we spotted a small village on the horizon. "Attack!"

Within minutes, the village was turned into a Saxon bloodbath. My ears rang with the cries of the Vikings and I was filled with the satisfaction of the raid.

Soon though, I noticed something was wrong. We were being pushed back. Far away, I saw figures in shining armour marching forward. Suddenly, I realised.

"Retreat!" I exclaimed, "The Normans have arrived!"

Ethan Yifan Wang (10)
Hilltop Academy, Summertown

START OF DESTRUCTION

In 1914, there was a group of assassins who were highly trained, highly skilled and most importantly, highly qualified. This group was called the Black Hand and they had one mission and one purpose: hunting down one man. Their mission was to assassinate Archduke Franz Ferdinand of Austria and Hungary. However, it wasn't going to be easy. Their first attempt was to silently throw a bomb. Amazingly, the driver dodged the bomb. The second attempt brought success when one man assassinated the Archduke and his wife in a public market!

Abhishek Vaghjee

Hilltop Academy, Summertown

MY EGYPTIAN DIARY

I was working in the hot sand when suddenly, the pharaoh arrived. It'd been a long time since I last saw the pharaoh, so I had to work extra hard all day.

When I could finally rest, I was given a tiny bit of food. It was mouldy bread. I hated the pharaoh. He treated us badly and was selfish. He never let us rest. It was a terrible day. The rest of the day, I dreamt about being the pharaoh. I would be kind to the whole kingdom and everyone would have their fair share of food and work.

Ian Zhang (9)
Hilltop Academy, Summertown

BUILDING THE GREAT WALL

I took my shirt off and strapped it around my waist. Sweat poured down my neck as I heaved a stone onto the strong structure. I saw the other men carrying a huge stone on their shoulders. They looked as fragile as a piece of glass. If I touched them, they would have broken into pieces. I ran to help but it was too late. The stone had overpowered them...

Eason Ying (10)
Hilltop Academy, Summertown

OTHER SIDE OF THE BEANSTALK

Nobody knew the truth about me. Behind the yellowing teeth and horrible hair, the tattered clothes and evil eyes, I was a loving husband, father, and now, to the excitement of all the giants, a grandfather. I was just the brutish barbarian who protected his gold out of greed - but what can I say? A giant's got to save for his pension too.

"Dear, come down for dinner."

Thoughts interrupted, yet I was grateful. Often, I would sit for hours and contemplate how I could have, should have, done something differently.

"It's human tonight, with BBQ."

Oh, my favourite...

Jack Sage (15)
Myton School, Warwick

KING GEORGE

The shadow of Mount Washington cloaked Yorktown in darkness. The rising sun behind the Virginian general's countenance basked him in divine light, characterising him as the deity we were always told he was. His steely gaze could be felt from all corners of the city: an eternal watchman keeping vigil. I tore my eyes away from the statue and refocused on the textbook. My eyes rushed across print, though I retained no information. After all, what was to learn? Page after page of praise for the man on the alabaster throne, the God King Washington, monarch of the American kingdom.

Samuel Evans (15)
Myton School, Warwick

POLAND'S REVENGE

I slammed myself into the coarse, dirt walls of the trench. A scream to my left. "Niemiecka szumowina!" A mortar shell plunged into the nearby earth. The wooden supports holding the ditch shattered, sending a splinter into my arm. Then I heard it. War gongs. Steeling my resolve, I pulled myself out of that cowardly hole and charged with fury alongside my Polish brethren. Blurs of white, grey, red and brown polluted my vision. An explosion of colours like a paint splatter. However, just like Adolf failed art school - he'd fail to take Poland today. Now he would pay.

Luke Latham
Myton School, Warwick

BUFF DUCK

He was buff. He was forced to live this way. Lifting weights for a total of ten minutes repaired the heartbreak and wrenching pain caused by his ex-girlfriend. Chugging the last of his pre-workout muscle gain shake, he swiftly moved onto bigger things. That was devouring his demon former beau. Shyly knocking on her door, he waited. An ominous creak radiated from the devil's lair and she appeared. He swallowed her up without a second thought.
"Job done, time for an ice cream."
He heard the terrific tune of an ice cream van and knew everything would be alright.

Luca Stafioiu
Myton School, Warwick

DR STRANGE

Doctor Strange serves as the Sorcerer Supreme, the primary protector of Earth against magical and mystical threats. Unable to accept this prognosis, he starts to travel the world searching for alternative ways of healing, which leads him to the ancient one, the Sorcerer Supreme. Strange becomes his student and learns to be a master of both mystical and martial arts. He acquires an assortment of mystical objects, including the powerful Eye of Agamotto and Cloak of Levitation, and takes up residence in a mansion referred to as the sanctum, New York City. He defends the world from mystical threats.

Cody Easterbrook (12)
Paignton Community Academy, Paignton

FNAF 3

Micheal was hired as a nightguard for the newest edition of FazBear Entertainment, this was the next step to finding the murderer, William Afton. Micheal hadn't seen him since he 'died', but he knew William was alive.

Night one, nothing. Night two, he saw him, William or SpringTrap. He was in the SpringBonnie suit, but it was rotted. You could see his flesh, it was a reddish-purple colour and it was pierced with metal parts. Micheal saw SpringTrap getting closer. He used his audio button to distract him, but it failed.

That night, he was murdered by his own father.

Talor Freeth (13)
Paignton Community Academy, Paignton

CHARLIE AND THE TERROR FACTORY

Charlie held his golden ticket tight and eagerly waited for the factory gates to open. The clock struck midnight and chimed loudly. The few lucky children entered the factory doors. Charlie suddenly felt very cold and shivers began to creep down his spine, something wasn't quite right. Charlie led the group through the narrow, darkened hall towards a door. He slowly opened it and peered through the gap. Charlie quickly shut the door and turned to the other children with a look of sheer horror on his face. Suddenly, the factory went into a dark lockdown. They were trapped!

Oliver Owston (11)
Paignton Community Academy, Paignton

IF THANOS WON

Thor, Iron Man and Captain America looked amazed as portals started to open and the superheroes came out! Maybe they could still win. Iron Man used his hand repulsors to soar towards Thanos but Thanos used his double-edged weapon to cut Iron Man in half. Captain America got angry and rushed towards him with Mjolnir but Thanos caught the hammer and hit Captain America with it. Thor came but Stormbreaker wasn't strong enough to cut through Thanos' skin. Thanos punched him so hard, it killed him. Hulk tried to use the gauntlet but Thanos took it and snapped his fingers.

Ryan Cornish (13)
Paignton Community Academy, Paignton

THE JEDI MASTER

At that moment, Anakin was ecstatic. He had been granted the rank of Jedi Master and was on the council! He loved the Order even more than before. However, it did make him a lot more arrogant due to his young age. He couldn't wait to share the news with Padme. After a while, he started noticing the senate disappearing from time to time. When this happened, Anakin crawled through the ventilation system and saw Palpatine on a call with the separatists. He immediately called the rest of the Republic and Palpatine was arrested. Afterwards, Anakin was given a medal.

Max Dunn (13)
Paignton Community Academy, Paignton

WRECK-IT RALPH: AN ISSUE IN THE SYSTEM

Ages ago when I was watching the race with Ralph, he said to me, "Felix, why did everything stop?" As this was unusual, I was puzzled but then we saw Vanellope's eyes change colour from her original eye colour to a light blue colour. Now, lots of people were hunting us, including Vanellope, Calhoun and King Candy. After making it to my house, we used vaccines to turn everyone back to normal but Vanellope was evading us. We had to hold her down and vaccinate her. Since then, we're all happy at the stadium since Vanellope won the grand prize.

Jayden Kilkenny (12)
Paignton Community Academy, Paignton

CHARLIE'S END

Charlie ran to the chocolate factory. He had found the golden ticket and was ecstatic! His parents were unsure if he should go, but his grandfather joined him and his parents mutually agreed. The gates to the factory were very tall and ornate, he stood frozen in awe. Charlie entered, followed by his grandpa and the others. Willy Wonka appeared, Charlie noticed blood on his jacket. He was too scared to point it out. They got to the first exhibition and the doors closed behind them. Willy grabbed Charlie and plunged a knife into his chest. It hit his heart.

Harrie Porter
Paignton Community Academy, Paignton

MINIONS WITH A TWIST

One day, Kevin, Stuart and Bob decided they needed a leader. So they left their cave and other Minions there. They all decided to go to New York.

When they arrived, they saw a concert. They decided to go there and met this wicked girl called Scarlet Overkill. Scarlet decided to let them into her house. Scarlet made Kevin, Stuart and Bob rob the Queen because she always wanted to be Queen herself. When the Minions stole the crown and realised that Scarlet was bad, they tried to get away. However, Scarlet didn't let them go and kept them forever.

Emily Walker (12)
Paignton Community Academy, Paignton

A TWISTED TALE

Kris was her name. Sitting alone on an eerie hill full of unkept grass, she believed she could see into the future and teleport anywhere she wanted. Her lasting wish was to see her mum. She therefore decided to put herself out there and tried to enter the past. However, her instincts told her that this was a bad option due to previous stories from those who had encountered bad experiences with monsters. She decided to ignore her conscience and went in anyway! Unfortunately, she got stuck in the dark bitter abyss, but did she see any monsters?

Ellie-Mae Knowles-Pease (15)
Paignton Community Academy, Paignton

DR STRANGE'S DREAM WALK

Dr Strange knew what he had to do. He had to dream walk! It was the only way to save America and the world. He gathered all the candles around him to form a circle and sat with his legs crossed ready to start the ritual. Before he started, he told Christine, "If they come for me, save me!" She nodded, unsure of what she was agreeing to. Dr Strange entered his deceased body from another universe and unhurried it. Using a magic spell, he got to the mountains ready to defeat the Scarlet Witch. Suddenly, the demons killed him.

Madi Bishop (12)
Paignton Community Academy, Paignton

BILL SIKES' ESCAPE

Oliver Twist had just found out that Nancy had been slaughtered in the alleyway. He hoped he wasn't next. Suddenly, sirens started to blare. Bill Sikes was on the run. He was causing havoc across the London skyline. He leapt from building to building.

When he was leaping from the canal building, the public thought he would finally be caught or fall to his death. Miraculously, he made the jump and no one could catch him. He was in his own league. He was never seen or heard of ever again. It was rumoured that he moved to another city.

David Pham (13)

Paignton Community Academy, Paignton

THE JOURNEY WE DON'T SEE

Moana is really not what you think but unfortunately, this young girl followed her dream and her grandma's passing wish to sail the sea and return the heart. On this journey she had been sent on, she got caught in a terrible storm and unfortunately didn't make it out alive. The story we see is actually Moana's journey to Heaven after her passing and the journey she had to go through to prove she was strong and her kind acts were to be part of Heaven called Te Fiti. That is how Moana healed Te Fiti with her pure soul.

Jacqueline Mclellan (15)
Paignton Community Academy, Paignton

THE LITTLE GOOD WOLF

The Little Good Wolf lived a nice life and was best friends with the Three Big Pigs who were very mean. He liked them very much and adored each of their three houses, wishing he could live in them.

One day, the pigs had a cunning idea. They planned to invite the wolf to dinner and blow his house down.

The wolf was delighted when he heard he could visit the pigs for dinner. The pigs blew down the wolf's house and he was so frustrated; he ate all three pigs greedily. He lived in their houses happily ever after.

Daniel Anthoney (13)
Paignton Community Academy, Paignton

THE BEANSTALK AND JACK

Jack was coming home with no food or money. He knew his mum was furious with him. As expected, his mum was livid. She threw beans everywhere and sent him to bed.

In the night, Jack heard a noise and wandered outside. He realised it was a massive beanstalk. He thought he could climb it, without knowing the dangers. There was a giant whose house was at the top of the stalk. He hated people climbing up, so when Jack was climbing up, he got a chainsaw. It went through like a knife through butter and the rest is history.

Mack Nettleton-Stokes (12)

Paignton Community Academy, Paignton

HARRY POTTER IN REVERSE

There once was a little boy who lived with his Aunt Petunia and Uncle Vernon. They lived on Privet Drive. Voldemort was forced to live under the stairs. It was very small and tight. Voldemort didn't have a mum or dad because they were killed when he was a baby by a man called Harry Potter. He scared Voldemort for life by killing his parents and giving him a scar that looked like a lightning bolt. He was never allowed out of his bedroom unless he wanted to go to the toilet, have his dinner or have something to eat...

Alfie Bradwell (12)
Paignton Community Academy, Paignton

THE MAGIC RIVER

Once upon a time a little boy, who lived in a rundown house in the middle of a forest, decided to go and explore. He always thought he could see stuff other people couldn't. When he set foot into the woods, he heard mysterious noises, but couldn't see anything in sight.

After a while, a magical river came out of nowhere and there was a character in a black cloak on a small wooden raft. The boy started to yell but nothing happened. All of a sudden, he got sucked into the floor. He was never heard of again.

Jacob Matthews (13)
Paignton Community Academy, Paignton

NEVERLAND

All the kids see me as the villain. Peter Pan makes me out to be the villain. Of course, Pan will always be the hero of this story. The kids believe he saved them but they're all wrong. Pan goes to orphanages and 'borrows' them. His little pixie helps him, she makes them forget it all. If you ever come to Neverland, you'll never go back. I once was one of these kids, but I grew up too quickly. I'll keep looking for the star, I don't know how long it'll take. Just please get me out of here.

Bryony Pearce (13)
Paignton Community Academy, Paignton

THE REAL KILLER

I suddenly found myself frozen still like a statue. Tears slowly poured. My hands began to tremble. The life drained out of my love. I could hear the sirens blaring in the distance. Finally, one of the detectives began to ask me questions. I started to describe to the detective a man in his late 30s who was dressed in a suit and top hat. He had a curly moustache and blue eyes. The police finally left me alone. I slowly smiled, knowing that I had just tipped the police in the opposite direction. No suspicion on me.

Erin Strong (13)
Paignton Community Academy, Paignton

TWISTED THINGS

Eleven and the gang were about to face the Demogorgon. El used her powers to try and exterminate the creature but failed and ended up passing out and letting the Demogorgon eat her. A member of the gang, Mike, ran to save El. He was too late, she was gone. He started to rage, then grabbed a lighter and burnt the Demogorgon to death. He then turned around and looked at the rest of the gang. Mike charged and slowly fought off everyone, one by one. He was on the rampage. He burnt the corpses and left the crime scene.

Kai Watson (13)
Paignton Community Academy, Paignton

THE UPSIDE DOWN BOYS

Tom and Hank sat in their house with their other friends but they had to go home, so they left. On the way home, Will took a turn and heard a sound. He ditched his bike and started running into the woods. Whatever the creature was, it snuck behind Will and tried to grab him. He continued running. As he sprinted home, he barged through the door but nobody was there. He ran back outside to grab a weapon but it was already too late. He and the monster had disappeared. His family looked for days but never found him.

Daynton Adams-Thompson (12)
Paignton Community Academy, Paignton

LABYRINTH TWIST

As Sarah realised the Goblin King had no power over her, she hoped for the best and thought of home, wishing she'd be back there once again. The time ran out and as she opened her eyes thinking she'd be snuggled up in her own bed, she saw the Goblin King holding a small goblin. This small goblin looked different to the others; this one was smaller and wore a red and white striped babygrow. And Sarah knew, this wasn't a bad dream trying to teach her to love her brother, it was reality.

Chloe Kerry (14)

Paignton Community Academy, Paignton

THE TWISTED TALE OF DOCTOR STRANGE

They never knew the truth about me. The truth about me is that I have secret powers that help me fly, shoot magical missiles and reverse time. I fight monsters from different universes who try to kill my friends or teammates. I try to save every one of my friends and comrades, but some of them die. I try to stop that from happening, but most of my friends and comrades die anyway. Maybe from disease or just old age. I can't just watch that, I have to kill my friends and comrades...

Harry Bulley (11)
Paignton Community Academy, Paignton

THREE LITTLE ERRORS

"I like your new house," the wolf whispered to himself, "But it'll be gone soon."
He strolled towards his rickety shed, conjuring a devious plan.
"A catapult! It's perfect, I'll destroy all three!"
Spending the following days tirelessly working, his catapult had enough power to destroy anything.
The day of destruction had arrived, and the wolf was ready. He'd been ready for weeks. He brought the catapult towards the sturdy structure and chuckled to himself - they were clueless! He readied his weapon, loading the ammo. At the last second, it all went wrong - the ammo fell and killed him.

Isabel Vale (14)
Shirebrook Academy, Shirebrook

ALICE IN MADLAND!

A giant purple caterpillar locked eyes on tiny Alice.
"Absalom?" Alice whispered.
The caterpillar cackled an evil laugh.
"Alice, is that who you are? You dare to disrespect my name?" he began to bellow as smoke billowed from his neon lips. "Nobody addresses me as that. The name is Big Caterpillar!" he roared in fury.
Alice glared in concern.
"What happened to you, Absalom?" Alice said, glaring at his now green tongue.
"It's not what happened to me, Al. It's what happened to you. We never changed, you changed us!"
She stared at the wet, cold grass in shame.

Bentley Mohammed (14)
Shirebrook Academy, Shirebrook

UNTANGLED

Flynn Rider was threading his fingers through Rapunzel's lengthy, brown hair. A sudden yell interrupted their time together. Carefully, they looked over the ledge and saw several guards peering around the tower to find the entrance. Fear flooded Rapzunel's senses because she knew that they wanted her hair. All of a sudden, they plunged through the window, barging Rapunzel to the side. Their knives searched for their target, Flynn Rider. He'd stolen the kingdom's crown and they'd arrived to retrieve it. Many knives were being slashed towards Flynn and Rapunzel threw her hair in defence. Brown hair dropped, turning blonde...

Maja Fidali (14)
Shirebrook Academy, Shirebrook

HOWL'S MOVING CASTLE

Sophie ascended the stairs, hair bouncing on her shoulders. Looking around, she noticed that the floor was littered with trinkets, clocks, gems, and items from Howl's room. Except for the infamous Howl, nothing had changed since she last visited.

"Howl? What exactly are you doing here?" Sophie approached the enigmatic figure in the corner, whispering softly.

As a reply, Howl ruffled his feathers and grunted. His human-like face contorted in pain, and his feathers contracted, leaving his arms bare. Sophie's face fell, and tears fell from her eyes as Howl breathed his last breath, his pain now over for eternity.

Sophie Ball (14)
Shirebrook Academy, Shirebrook

TANGLED

"Rapunzel, let down your hair!"
I heard him climb up, silently wishing he hadn't. My 'mother' threw my hair down while I was trying to escape the chains around my hands, trying to scream as nothing came out of my mouth.
"You're lucky it wasn't you, Rapunzel."
Her hands reached around Eugene's neck, grabbing him tightly and pulling him in whilst reaching into her pockets.
"Mother, no!" I screamed.
She pulled her hand back, stabbing Eugene with her dagger. His body lost all life and he fell into my vanity mirror, instantly breaking it. Eugene was dead.

Demi-Leigh Harvey (14)
Shirebrook Academy, Shirebrook

ALICE IN MADLAND

"She's late, she's late! Alice, where are you? You should be here."

Those were the words I remember saying before everything, everything, *everything* changed. "Where is she? She's, she's late!"

Why is this happening? She is here, she's always here. Same time every day, never late. Now we have all changed, I can't control myself. Why am I like this? Everything has to be perfect, but who am I kidding? Nothing is perfect anymore. I know the queen did it, it's all her fault. What, what is this feeling inside my mind? My brain, it hurts. *Help!*

Jennifer McIntyre (14)
Shirebrook Academy, Shirebrook

THE LITTLE END OF RIDING HOOD

The crunch and crackle of the ground below and the pants and huffs of the big dangerous wolf approaching enveloped the girl's little heart. The bubbling, bursting foam of necessity covered the fangs that killed so many helpless victims.

"Help, help!" echoed through the wood.

The splintering, shattering screams of pain made all the heroes shiver. The gushing river flowed from her face like her crimson hooded cape. Her hair grew longer and all over her body, teeth like the wolf attacking her before, her eyes grew yellow and her heart grew cold. *Aroooo!*

This was how Little Red died.

Harrison Robson (14)

Shirebrook Academy, Shirebrook

THE DOGS AND THE DRAGON

I suddenly found myself face to face with three little dogs. I didn't know where they came from. I was only out for a little walk in the woods.

"Where are you going?" I asked them curiously.

"We're going to build some houses. I'm going to make mine out of straw," said the littlest of the dogs.

"Straw? That's a terrible idea. You should use stone," I said, "Or they'll fall down in the breeze."

The dogs said, "Okay."

Later, a dragon tried to eat the dogs. He couldn't get past their houses. Then the dragon died of hunger.

Axel Steers (12)
Shirebrook Academy, Shirebrook

PETER AND WENDY

"Peter?"

"Wendy, you weren't supposed to see this."

I love him, I really do, but here he is in front of me, covered in blood; I fell in love with a psychopath.

"What did you do?"

"Wendy, darling, I did this for us..."

"Us? They did nothing, they loved you!"

"But I have to stay young with you, it's the only way."

Tears fall from his eyes. I walk closer, I love him after all, embracing him in a hug. The knife pierces his skin, the blood covers my hand. I'll love him in death. Till death do us part.

Ella Murcott (14)

Shirebrook Academy, Shirebrook

IF HITLER WON THE WAR

It was a normal day until I turned on my radio. It said, "Hitler's won the war!"
"Oh no!" I said, almost crying. I was so scared, I couldn't move. I suddenly found myself in a Nazi camp.
"Oh my god!" I screamed.
I was in the Nazi camp because I had special needs.
"Hi, do you know a way out of here?" I whispered to an English soldier.
"No, but we can make a plan. Also, Hitler's ordered the execution of all people with special needs, so we must hurry!"
We escaped... but barely, with our lives!

Braydon Johnson (12)
Shirebrook Academy, Shirebrook

HER SAVIOUR

Belle met him two weeks ago. She loved him dearly; his azure eyes, his copper hair. He saved her. He brought her tea every day; gave her food every day; he wasn't like the others. Every time Belle saw him, it brought her to tears just how kind he was. Adam was the only one who didn't find her insane. Every evening, he'd leave as she tried to cling onto him, crying. One day, he didn't come back...

"I don't want her case, she's obsessed!" he professed to his supervisor.

"You're the only one who can save her," she retorted.

Kornelia Kandyba (13)
Shirebrook Academy, Shirebrook

OF MICE AND MEN 2

Calm, clear water flowed past as Lennie hid in the bushes. George caught up with Lennie and devised a cunning plan. Curly ran, wielding a revolver. Curly, however, was stupid, holding his gun like a maniac. George laid out a log. Curly stumbled down. George lined his sights with Curly's head. 3, 2, 1... *Bang!* The piercing sound rattled through the woods, splitting trees in half. Birds fled from the scene like people at the end of rock concerts.

A few seconds later, the cry of a dead man rang amongst the animals roaming around. Curly was riddled with death!

Joshua Lewin (14)

Shirebrook Academy, Shirebrook

LOST AT SEA

We've been waiting for two weeks for her to come home. The darkness is spreading, getting stronger, killing our fish, poisoning our coconuts. Nothing's left, except hope. The atmosphere around us is becoming more and more polluted every day; my breaths are running out; possibly my hope as well. The leaves on our once evergreens have turned brown, our grass that was once healthy is slowly dying, what once used to be our daytime is now our night-time. Our time on this island is slowly coming to an end. If Moana doesn't come home soon, we're all going to die.

Alexa Baker (13)
Shirebrook Academy, Shirebrook

IT WAS ALL A DREAM

The big day had arrived. It was time for Peter to graduate. He jumped out of bed and hopped into his best clothes. Peter had just picked up his tie when his 2001 police scanner sprung into life! He didn't even know it still worked. It announced the words: "Dispatch all units downtown, I can't explai-" Peter sighed and stared at his red suit. Peter quickly changed clothes and hopped onto his balcony. "The city needs me," he said before launching himself off the ledge. He began to feel ill, dizzy and tired. Soon, he was falling. He woke up.

Gabriel Rodgers (12)
Shirebrook Academy, Shirebrook

THE LAKE

I'm sitting in the woods revising for a test, listening to the birds tweet. It's about 9:00pm and I'm about to walk home. I keep hearing ghostly screams! Tomorrow's Halloween. I come across a lake with grimy plastic bottles floating around and water snakes fishing for food. I feel something brush against my leg. I look down... nothing. As I walk closer to the lake, I see a shadow and a baby crying in fear. The baby's in a flimsy wooden basket floating down the lake, making its way towards the waterfall. I jump in and something drags me down!

Kacie Boulton (13)
Shirebrook Academy, Shirebrook

THE STALKER BESIDE THE ROAD

It's Saturday night, October 31st - Halloween. You're trick or treating down Death Street. You knock on your friend's door. No answer. You go home and knock. No answer. You bang on the windows and see a figure walking towards the door. You hide. You see a tall man who you can only assume is your dad, but you have no hope. You march closer to the door thinking it's your dad, but it's unexplainable. You've no choice but to go inside the house. You sneak down the corridor and hear a noise in the kitchen. You go to encounter death...

Enoch Donkor (13)
Shirebrook Academy, Shirebrook

THE CHOCOLATE MACHINE!

I'd never felt conscious about my weight until then. I was stuck in the chocolate tube, alone with no help. Everyone laughed. I screamed out, "Help, help!" but nothing changed. I was drenched in a brown liquid whilst stranded but finally, I moved up. The only thing was, I hadn't escaped. I was moving in a loop; left, right, left, right. I screamed at the top of my lungs. It felt like I was on a roller coaster. Suddenly, I started falling. I wasn't in the tube anymore. I heard a splash underneath me. I was in a chocolate machine...

Roxy Key (11)

Shirebrook Academy, Shirebrook

THE LIGHTHOUSE

As the storm raged on, I desperately rushed back and forth from the lighthouse to my home checking on my friend's condition and keeping the light on so they'd leave us alone. *I've just gotta make it till dawn and they'll be gone. Then I'll be able to get my friend's help and we'll never talk about this night or ever touch that damned book.* This was supposed to be a relaxing getaway, not this mess. *No, no, no! Oh God, please no! The light has gone out. I have to relight it but what about them?* Wait, no, st-

Hope Sykes (13)
Shirebrook Academy, Shirebrook

MIKE

"All we need now are the names of your men," he told me, assuming I'd still be loyal.

"I'd advise you to leave town and never come back. The DEA's coming down on us hard since you had to go and kill Fring," I admitted to him, but wasn't finished.

"You just had to be the man, didn't you? If you'd done your job and known your place, we-"

Before I could finish, he shot me in a motion so subtle, I missed it. Maybe I was too angry to notice. He had probably made up his mind ages ago.

Owen Thorpe (14)

Shirebrook Academy, Shirebrook

NEMO

3rd of July, 1992. The day hell broke loose in the family. Nemo was nowhere to be seen. The last time he was spotted was the night before. Everything seemed normal the night before. Little did they know, tragedy was about to come. Nemo's door had been suspiciously left wide open, without him inside. Not only was this strange, but there was nothing left inside. All of his belongings had suddenly disappeared without making a sound. Everyone was panicking, nobody knew what to do or why this happened until they checked under the bed. Nemo was dead.

Oliver Hough (14)
Shirebrook Academy, Shirebrook

SNOW WHITE AND THE EVIL DWARVES

Snow White came across seven dwarves whilst going on a midnight stroll. They seemed so bubbly and talkative. As she started to talk to them more, she got invited around their house. When she arrived, it was a small modern cottage with a Range Rover outside. As Snow entered the cottage, they locked the door and started acting strangely. They were whispering to each other and being ever so quiet. Suddenly, Snow White got hit around the head with a plate. Glass went all over the place, causing her head to bleed non-stop. Sadly, she then passed away.

Lillie Mower (13)
Shirebrook Academy, Shirebrook

HOPE

I couldn't believe my eyes - seven small ferrets, their mum had died. My neighbours bred ferrets, yet this wasn't normal. I kept them alive and picked one to keep. We formed a bond and I even named her Hope. Sadly, the others began dying and only Hope lived. I fed her and she was so close to opening her eyes. She was very healthy and had a high chance of living.

Unfortunately, one morning, she passed away. I buried her and planted poppies on her grave, as when she was born, poppies flowered. When she died, the poppy seeds spread.

Lucy Williams (12)
Shirebrook Academy, Shirebrook

THE BATTLE OF HEAVEN

One Sunday morning in 1266, the bell was screaming in my ear. I woke up as confused as ever. I saw my army marching out of the kingdom. I looked over the beach; the Jewish Empire were marching towards my kingdom. There must've been 200,000, nearly 300,000 of them. I grabbed my armour, sword and knife. I ran out and got anyone who could fight. We needed several people to win this battle. I gathered as many resources as I could. I commanded the archers to fire at the enemy. They blocked them all, not one died. *We're gonna lose.*

Logan Middleton (14)
Shirebrook Academy, Shirebrook

ALICE IN MADLAND

Nobody knew the truth about me - the Queen of Hearts. Alice, a treasonous little girl, had been poisoned by me. A few moments ago, she stole some of my delicious jam tarts and was caught in the act by one of the guards. She needed punishment. Whilst Alice protested her innocence, I found a reasonable punishment for her treason - a drink of poison. She would have this potion after we had a little match of croquet. If she won, she would live. If she lost, she would drink the poison - she lost. Now she's lying here on the ground, dead...

Abigail Holmes (14)
Shirebrook Academy, Shirebrook

CLIFFORD THE BIG RED DOG

They'd just left the house leaving Clifford unattended. This was their first time leaving him. They went shopping. All of a sudden, there was a knock at the door. It was the postman. Clifford was scared. He jumped through the wall and mauled him. The postman lay on the floor in a pool of blood. Clifford liked what he'd just done and went on a spree. His first stop was the shop he visited every morning. He never liked the shopkeeper because he was always mean-spirited to him. So he decided to crush the shop and him along with it.

Joshua Kirk (14)
Shirebrook Academy, Shirebrook

THE HORROR OF SLEEPING BEAUTY

Once upon a time, there was a pretty woman. Her mum mysteriously died when she was a young girl. Her father was a rich man. There was a very handsome man on the other side of the village who all the girls wanted. He only wanted Aurora, but everything took a mysterious turn...
A random old woman met Aurora in the woods. Out of nowhere, a mysterious creature came out of the trees. News spread around that the princess was missing. The prince looked in the woods and mysteriously found her covered in the leaves and crunchy thorns. Dead.

Ciara Wormall (12)
Shirebrook Academy, Shirebrook

THE NOT VERY BRIGHT BMXER

Milosz was a pro-BMXer then something happened...
He was just riding his bike on the track when this scary man wearing a big black coat and a tall black hat from the 70s went up to him and opened his coat.
He said, "Do u want some potions to make u faster?"
Milosz said, "Yes."
Later that day, the young boy drank the potion.
On race day, he drank it again and his belly hurt in the middle of the race. Suddenly, he turned into a monster and he nearly died. Then, all of a sudden, he did die.

Harley Buckingham (13)
Shirebrook Academy, Shirebrook

FROZEN

It was a normal day until Anna and Elsa got woken up by their parents because it was Elsa's coronation. Elsa didn't want to be queen, but she didn't want her parents to know that. She didn't just have ice power, she also had fire power. That night, Anna was happy for Elsa to be queen but when Anna went to Elsa's bedroom, she was gone. Elsa had run away. She told her parents. They searched for her everywhere but there was no sign.

Two years later, they found her, but they died as soon as they got there.

Kaitlyn Hutchinson-Price (12)
Shirebrook Academy, Shirebrook

ALICE IN MADLAND

Bright. Too bright. I start to open my eyes, allowing myself to see two people in white coats.

Wait. Where am I? How did I get here? I think to myself.

I try to breathe in, causing a burning pain to erupt in my chest. My vision blurs as I turn my head, recognising two figures standing next to my bed. My parents. My memory is fuzzy, I remember going down the rabbit hole. The potion glows unusually. I drink it. There is a burning sensation in my chest. I black out. Now I see the blue caterpillar from Wonderland...

Ava Shaw (14)
Shirebrook Academy, Shirebrook

FALLING BUT FLYING CARPET

Soaring through the sky, cold air blowing in my face, the ride began to get bumpy. The speed started picking up as I shot into the air. I could feel the clouds in-between my fingers and then: a world of darkness with sparkly stars. The carpet started shaking, so I held on tight. Twisting and spinning in the air, the carpet shook and I let go... Dropping from extreme heights wasn't the best way to meet your end. As I felt my insides dropping and my view shaking, I hit the floor. I couldn't feel anything and my sight went.

Tilly Starkey (13)
Shirebrook Academy, Shirebrook

MATILDA

"Bruce Bogtrotter!" screamed Miss Trunchbull.
He stood up and walked trembling towards the stage.
Footsteps echoed as the cook came from behind the curtain with a chocolate cake twice the size of Bruce's head. His face dropped when Miss Trunchbull demanded he ate it all and to make sure there were no crumbs left. He submerged his face into the cake and the sweet sensation of the chocolate touched his mouth and made him want to eat more. One last bite. His eyes widened and Bruce fell to the floor and died.

Jessica Shipman (14)
Shirebrook Academy, Shirebrook

DUSTIN'S LOVE STORY

Dustin Henderson was en route to his summer camp destination. It was a small camp focused on engineering and science. His walkie-talkie was prepared for use when he returned home to connect with Will, Mike and Lucas. When he met a female who was equally intelligent and attractive to him, he had no idea how his life would change. He was working on the slammer, an automatic hammer, and the Cerebro, a ham radio, when Suzie, a girl who was a genius in every sense of the word, came walking over and he adored her upon first sight.

Lillie Hunt (14)
Shirebrook Academy, Shirebrook

MOANA: A TWISTED TALE

Sailing across the open ocean, Moana was only metres away from Te Fiti. Her heart began to race as the once calm, gentle waves became aggressive punches on the boat's side. The boat began to sway from side to side, making her lose her balance and topple headfirst into the sea. Panicking, she forgot how to swim, half expecting the sea to help her out. She began shouting for Maui but it was too late, the waves had her in their grasp and she couldn't escape. She felt her last breaths slip away and her body went limp.

Teigan Gascoigne (14)
Shirebrook Academy, Shirebrook

WE GO, JIM!

Once upon a time, there was a skinny Xbox gamer with the nickname of Cbum. His real name was Chris Bumstead and he wasted his teenage life away playing Fall Guys with his friends. His high school relationship had just come to an end and Cbum was feeling irate. He saw a few things about the gym and decided he would try it out. He rapidly gained muscle and he began watching a legend by the name of Zyzz. Fast forward 25 years and Cbum is a triple Mr Olympia winner for classic physique. That's why he's the G.O.A.T.

Lucas Thomas (14)
Shirebrook Academy, Shirebrook

SLEEPING RUMOURS

The tower looked the same as always. Inside, lay a woman who had been asleep for years. No one knew how this had happened to her. The rumour was that the only way to wake her up was to place a kiss upon her lips. One brave soul came upon this tower and was intrigued as to what was inside. Upon entering, he was met with the woman sleeping. He had heard the rumours and kissed her, then waited for her to awake but instead of waking, she lay still. He had come all this way for nothing but disappointment.

Faye Newton (14)
Shirebrook Academy, Shirebrook

JACK AND JILL

Jack and Jill didn't go down the hill to fetch a pail of water. Jill fell down and broke her musty old crown. Then Jack ran down so fast after her. As Jack went down the hill, he tripped over his feet and fell over. He dropped to the floor and broke his nose. Blood popped out and *boom!* He face-planted the floor. Jill got up feeling bruised. Her knees were bloody and scabby. Half of her skin was peeled off and then the floor was scabby. There was just a pile of dead skin on the floor.

Isabelle Tipple
Shirebrook Academy, Shirebrook

MY TIME AT CHUCK E. CHEESE

I went to Chuck E. Cheese for my birthday. I went to the counter to get some tokens and I got 20 tokens to win prizes. My food wasn't coming out for a couple of hours, so I played on most of the arcade machines and lost track of time. My mum shouted at me to go and get my food. Before I tucked in, I saw a kid walk up to the animatronics and put his hand in. But before he could take it out the mouth, it closed and dragged him through the curtain to a blood-covered room...

Tyler Buxton (14)
Shirebrook Academy, Shirebrook

HARRY POTTER AND THE GREAT BETRAYAL

The plan is in motion. It is finally my time to strike. I am Harry Potter and when I was very young, the Dark Lord, Lord Voldemort, struck me with his magic, never to be seen again. I am now thirteen and going back to Hogwarts School as a Slytherin. This time, I am going to kill Dumbledore to obtain his hand and bring back Lord Voldemort once again. It is time for me to win. I am going to take him to the Chamber of Secrets and order the Basilisk to strike him right there.

Brandon Sherwood (14)
Shirebrook Academy, Shirebrook

THE CONJURING REVERSED

My plan was in action. I had made people think that I lived in the house to provoke the spirit when really all I did was try to free the house of the demonic spirit that was tormenting the family that owned the house. The demon's name was Bathsheba Sherman. I had exorcised the man's wife that had unfortunately been possessed by the demonic spirit, but in the end, I failed.

Weeks later, the man's wife had had enough and she committed suicide.

Carter Laker (13)
Shirebrook Academy, Shirebrook

FIVE STREET

I finished boring school, but to get home, I had to go down Five Street which was not a good place to walk. I saw my teacher and said hi, but he didn't reply. He slowly walked up to me, so I ran home but I lost my key. There was no way to get in as my dad was at work. My maths teacher got closer. I always thought he was a creep. My dad finally came home, just before my teacher got there. It went quiet. My dad got killed. He said I was next...

Milly Merrington (13)
Shirebrook Academy, Shirebrook

PRINCE CHARMING

"Prince Charming took advantage of his power to find Cinderella."

Prince Charming jumped up, frantically. "Objection!"

"On what grounds?" questioned the judge, with an eyebrow arch.

"I'm royalty, I'm allowed. There is no rule objecting it," stuttered Prince Charming

"That means nothing in court. Continue prosecution," stated the judge.

"Did Cinderella leave her slipper on purpose? Was she trying to escape to get away from you?"

Prince Charming's censurable eyes were glaring at Cinderella in the distance.

"Prince Charming took advantage of his position, harassment, so I sentence him to 20 years with no royal status," announced the judge.

Sophie Smith (14)
The Highcrest Academy, High Wycombe

THE FATE OF THE PERFECT PORRIDGE

Bang! Eyes open. Heart racing. Stomach churning. I was thrust onto the kitchen counter, unsure of my fate. We were separated, just like that. Our hearts shattered. We cascaded into different bowls and scolding hot torture was added, finishing off the mix. Then those torturous bears, the big brown bullies, just left, leaving us neglected. And as for that girl! "Ooh, it's too hot! Too cold!" I could sense it coming as part of my being was gobbled up. "Ah, just right."
Seeing the black tube coming closer, I took one last breath as the world blacked out.

Naomi Lyon
The Highcrest Academy, High Wycombe

FAIRY GOD-WITCH

Once upon a bloomin' time, I was summoned by a tearful girl covered in cinders. Looking at me, she asked, "Are you my fairy godmother?" *Not again*, I thought. How many times did I have to tell people I was an evil witch! The girl kept talking about wicked sisters and a dusty cellar. I would've said no if I could get a word in. I said the only thing I could to get her to be quiet.

"Yes, I'm your fairy godmother! You shall go to the ball."
I guessed it wouldn't hurt to play along just once.

Saarah Mahmood (14)
The Highcrest Academy, High Wycombe

KING JULIAN

I was at a party, all of the animals were there; Alex, Gloria, the zebra, I can't remember his name but he's irrelevant right now. Then, I saw Maurice out of the corner of my eye. Oh, dancing bananas, he was looking a little too fine, the power of the samba. Oh, his hips, they shook like maracas (he's still not as good as me though). I don't know what happened, but the next thing I remember is the soft sensation of Maurice's lips on mine and the sweet smell of bananas. Pure heaven, the rest is history.

Gemma Eames
The Highcrest Academy, High Wycombe

THE THIRD PIG

I hated my brothers; I was the least favourite pig. One day, our mother couldn't care for us anymore, so we had to leave. I was offered straw and bricks to make my house, but I refused. However, my brothers accepted and laughed at me as they had houses and I didn't. Yesterday, a man offered me bricks. I accepted and built my house.
One day, a wolf came along and tried to blow all our houses down. My brothers' houses were all blown down and they were gobbled up. With my brick house, I watched smugly.

Leah Mills
The Highcrest Academy, High Wycombe

CARL THE CLOWN

One Halloween, Carl was walking around knocking on doors. No answer. Everyone ran away from him. Carl just wanted to be liked. "Hi, are you okay?" asked Tom.
Surprised, Carl looked up.
"Why aren't you running away from me?" questioned Carl.
"Why would I?" asked Tom.
"Because I'm ugly," added Carl.
"Don't say that! Everyone is unique in their own way," said Tom. "Look, why don't you and me go trick or treating?"
"Really? Thanks so much!" exclaimed Carl.
His face lit up with happiness.
After that day, nobody hated Carl. He made loads of new friends. It was amazing.

Oscar Field (12)
Wellington School, Timperley

TEST ONE

"Huh?" I said, panicking.

"Yeah, you ready for test one?"

"You bet."

Bang! A massive shockwave burst through the atmosphere. Amongst the mysterious mist, three pigs stood.

"Huh? Who are you?" the bacon-filled one asked.

"Tim, Tam and Tom. War!"

"What?"

Suddenly, numerous wolves commenced from the large hill I was on. *Bang! Wallop! Pew!*

"Ugh!" I groaned.

Tom was doing a lot better than anyone else. The mist was too strong.

"Help!" Tim screamed.

I slowly got up. I found a dung cannon the pigs made. But no, a wolf struck me in my chest.

Ryan Pickup

Wellington School, Timperley

GRANDBOMB VS BEIGHTON THE BENEVOLENT

There was once a small town in Blocksville where a remarkable young fellow named GrandBomb lived. GrandBomb's mission in life was to kill Beighton the evil wizard. So GrandBomb and his crew went to kill him. The next day, GrandBomb and his minions set off to kill Beighton. They marched through the magical forest and swam through the lake. Soon, they reached Beighton's castle made of quartz. Beighton had a huge army; it wasn't powerful enough. GrandBomb fly-kicked everyone and shot arrows at the guards. His minions sprayed Beighton with candy canes and GrandBomb blew up the castle. They'd won.

Arthur Finney (14)
Wellington School, Timperley

SCARLET OVERKILL'S BACKSTORY

The plan is in motion. I'll be queen! I'll make Britain great again! Finally, I'll not need to dream about ruling the world, it'll be reality now. Make rumours about Queen Lizzy and that will be it. As long as those pesky Minions don't ruin my presentation, we'll be all good. My marriage is today. The Minions are locked away, we're fine.

"You may kiss the bride."

No! The Minions have escaped! They're ruining it. Them yellow predators are ruining my future. No! Boris Johnson announces I will not be Queen. It'll be Bob the Minion instead. Revenge is on!

James Barnes (12)
Wellington School, Timperley

THE PRINCE'S REGRET

Bang! The clock struck eleven. I saw her face change into surprise as she stepped away from me.

My princess' sapphire dress was stripped away, piece by piece.

Thousands of beady eyes stared over at us. Left clothed in rags of pink and barefoot, she stood in my Ballroom.

I couldn't look, I couldn't see what I mustn't have. This was for my Kingdom, I mustn't think of myself with marriage.

She stared at me.

My father stared at me wondering what I'd do.

I sent her away, I had to, for my Kingdom.

That's what I've been telling myself.

Amy Fielding (13)

Wellington School, Timperley

HOOK'S BATTLE

"Sir, sir!" exclaimed Smee.

"What?" muttered Captain Hook.

"He's back again," said Smee.

Then suddenly, Captain Hook had a flashback and started thinking of the time he was abducted by Peter Pan. He thought he was loved but no, he was manipulated by the one he called a friend.

So later that night, he went to the docks with his crew. He left on his boat. They laughed and thanked Hook but Hook still felt his presence. Peter Pan was still with them but not where he could be seen. They duelled and Hook had to give up his arm.

Mason Onyemem (13)
Wellington School, Timperley

MY VENGEANCE

Lurking in the nyctophobic darkness, I grasped my blade, waiting for Hermes to amble by. Suddenly, I withdrew my fierce weapon and beheaded the now-deceased god. Lightning struck the halls of the gods. Water flooded and seeped into every crack and crevice. Blood spurted and encased me, suffocating, drowning, withering all it touched. I knew the gods would be angered, but my hatred and vengeance forced me to push forward towards the gods. I felt the scalding of water and the electricity of lightning burning upon me and as I was falling, I remembered one thing; my dead father.

Sufyaan Farid (14)
Wellington School, Timperley

SINKING SHADOW

As they flew over the glittering ocean underneath the shining sky, Wendy was overjoyed to inform her mother about this wild adventure. The second star to the right was within reaching distance when she felt a strong tug pulling her back. Her facial expression changed as her brothers left her sight. She glanced down to see a sly and scary shadow weighing her down. Drowning in an ocean of fear, the mermaids cackled. Without Peter, she would lead a darker fate than Captain Hook. Crocodile food! As she sank deeper, her breaths became slower until they completely stopped.

Alice Stephens (13)
Wellington School, Timperley

HUMPTY DUMPTY

Seven hundred and thirty-four days I'd been stuck on this cursed wall, just waiting and wishing for an opportunity to get down when suddenly, a magical rope appeared from the sky leading to the almighty ground. *A gift from the gods?* I thought. Without hesitation, I took my chance and leapt down from the wall and landed on the rope. Unfortunately, the rope began to fall apart as I started my descent! Before I knew it, the rope beneath my hands had snapped and fallen by all odds. But luckily, a brave horse appeared to save me from inevitable death!

Elijah Lyttle (13)
Wellington School, Timperley

THE WOLF: THE TRUE STORY

I suddenly found myself in a horrible situation. I was strolling through the woods when I spotted something far away. It was Little Red Riding Hood. I thought to myself, *She must be visiting Granny*, who happened to be a very good friend of mine. I headed to her cabin to say hello. That's when I noticed something strange. Someone was pretending to be Granny. By this time, Little Red had reached the path. I acted on instinct. I broke down the door and ate the intruder to protect Little Red Riding Hood. That's how I became a hated villain.

Joe Tan (12)
Wellington School, Timperley

THE BEAST

A dull yellow eye opens in front of me. I turn around, run. *Run!* Flames shoot up, causing me to stop...
Trapped in a ring of fire with this beast: my heart pounds, my legs shake, my breathing intensifies; panic really sets in when this 'thing' stands up. Starting to creep towards me, it hisses and snarls at me as if to say, leave.
Smoke starts to fill my lungs as I start to see the black, scaly creature clearer. It's like it has no face. Purple teeth sticking out of its... chest? And then...
It all went black.

Neve Henderson (14)
Wellington School, Timperley

LITTLE RED

One day, there was a girl called Little Red Riding Hood. She was on her way to her grandma's house. When she arrived, she looked through the window. She saw her grandma being eaten alive by a wolf. She walked in and saw the wolf wearing her grandma's clothes in bed.

She said, "Hi, Grandma. You look different."

The wolf said, "Come here so I can eat you."

She pulled out a rifle and shot the wolf. She opened its body to look for her grandma, but she was already gone. So she burnt the house and the wolf.

Joseph Turner (13)
Wellington School, Timperley

LITTLE RED RIDING HOOD

I suddenly found myself waking up lying on a cushion of plants and flowers. A wolf approached me. I wasn't sure how to act! The wolf helped me up and explained his plan. I picked up a beautiful bouquet and began to follow the cobbly road to Grandma's cottage.

When we arrived at Grandma's cottage, I handed her the beautiful bouquet and she offered us some muffins. I slipped the knife down my sleeve and stabbed her. She stared at me. She was terrified. By the time Mum arrived, me and the wolf ran to safety. Safe from the blame!

Isabelle Taylor (13)
Wellington School, Timperley

THE OGRE'S JOURNEY

It was a normal day in Britain until a large, green, ugly ogre got a letter through the door saying he had been hand-picked by Prime Minister Farquaad to assist Ukraine in the war against Russia. So he grabbed his essentials and set off on the long distance through deserts and mountains, land and sea. The ogre found himself outside a stranded, rotten, isolated shack. Around the corner of this shack was a tied-up donkey. He untied him and they seemed to get along. So the donkey helped the Ogre. When they arrived, the ogre got shot and killed.

Zak Adams (13)
Wellington School, Timperley

I DIDN'T REALISE

I sprinted through the dull forest. Just like me, it soon turned dull and grey. A thick smog blanketed the dead land. A thin beam of light illuminated a small colourful house located on a hill. I ran and ran and ran. I arrived at the house. Inside, a small pig wandered around. I couldn't contain my excitement. Finally, someone not affected by the world. The pig looked at me and squealed. I believed we were playing a game. Soon, I noticed when I breathed, the house shuddered. I took a deep breath. That was that. Only the smog remained.

Benjamin Mudd (13)
Wellington School, Timperley

IF THE SHOE FITS

It was two days after the ball and it'd been a relentless search since. I felt like I'd searched high and low for my Cinderella, but now my carriage carried me into the rougher part of town. All the girls were lined up, hoping that the shoe would fit onto their foot. As soon as they all saw me approach, they screamed in excitement.

About 30 minutes later, the shoe had fit most of the girls' feet. One of them fit into the slipper but she looked poorer than my Cinderella. Defeated, I walked away from her, not knowing more.

Lola Brumby (13)
Wellington School, Timperley

ROMEO AND JULIET'S DREAM

Romeo's lips were about to touch the potion when the love of his life, Juliet, awoke. He was stunned. He dropped the potion and went to hug Juliet as quick as he could. Romeo started to cry and couldn't believe his eyes. Was he in a dream? He was baffled, but he couldn't care less. All he wanted was just a glance at her. He was crying with happiness; living his best life. Juliet was very tired, still suffering from the potion's after-effect and didn't know if she was dead or alive. But they survived and that was that.

Daniel Lamb (13)
Wellington School, Timperley

THE TRUTH

Nobody would've known the truth. Joyfully, Rapunzel and I hugged each other, celebrating the death of Mother Gothel. Her embrace was as warm as the sun; her cheeks lit up like lanterns. Poor girl. She didn't know what the future had in store for her. Groaning and moaning, she looked up at me like a confused puppy. Rapunzel had looked down to see her crimson juice pouring out. Why? You ask. It was all part of the plan. Revenge is a dish that is always best served cold. You didn't actually think Mother Gothel was dead, did you?

Emaan Humayun (14)
Wellington School, Timperley

IT WAS ALL PART OF THE PLAN

I was freaking out as I charged into the abandoned warehouse. But little did he know, it was all part of the plan. I ordered my henchman to get the beam of death. "Minion, now!" The beam struck the hero who was struggling to escape. Me and my Minion witnessed the decoy warehouse blowing up, but then he came after us. We ran around in circles. The hero landed on me. I started bellowing and got him off... We were in shock. It was a skeleton! "We won! We can do whatever we want!" Many thoughts came to my mind.

Jacob Cleevely (12)
Wellington School, Timperley

AUSCHWITZ

Me and my family were going to a place called Auschwitz because of my dad's job. Once we got there, I started to walk through the woods. Then I started to see fences.
"Hello?" a skinny boy said.
Then I replied, "Who are you?"
"My name is Shmuel, do you have any food?" he said.
As I climbed over the fence to give him the food, I realised that something felt wrong. *Bash!* It was too late, I fell into the trap. The last thing I saw was Shmuel on top of me wrestling me to the ground.

Seiji Ivison (13)
Wellington School, Timperley

ZAZU: LONG LIVE THE KING

Nobody knows what really happened. Mufasa stole the throne from Scar. He should've been the king. I hate having to fly around for Mufasa, I should be working with Scar. It's all because of his son, Simba. Just because he is a great heir, doesn't mean Scar shouldn't be the king. Yes, Scar has a massive, scary army that has probably killed birds like me and would've shown dominance to the land for years to come. Not just one heir, but a whole army. I don't want to follow Mufasa, I want Scar. Long live the king.

Thomas Weilding (14)
Wellington School, Timperley

CAPTAIN HOOK'S HOGWARTS BATTLE

Captain Hook stole a wand from Hogwarts. He didn't show up until years later. Voldemort was now fully trained and strong, so he would be ready for Captain Hook's presence. Harry Potter wasn't however. *Bang!* Captain Hook's troops stormed the place and the battle had begun.

After some time, many had died. Voldemort battled Captain Hook and eventually won. Captain Hook turned into dust and lost. However, Voldemort was heavily injured.

After three months, he finally recovered and Harry Potter died.

Calico Kee (13)
Wellington School, Timperley

THE WITCH: HANSEL AND GRETEL

Nobody knew the truth about me. I was portrayed as the villain. But am I? The story starts when I was younger... My mum owned a bakery. She used to make loads of delicious treats. She was loved by everyone and so was I, until one day, the villagers grew jealous of how much money she was making and burnt down our bakery. That's why I wanted to get revenge. That's why my hair's grey from the ashes, my face wrinkled from the trauma. So am I a witch or misunderstood? However, I got revenge on the villagers' children.

Isabelle-Louise Salinger (13)
Wellington School, Timperley

URSULA'S TRADE

Nobody knew the truth about me... I just desperately wanted to be pretty like Ariel. One day, I 'unexpectedly' came across her and I traded my legs for her hair and voice. I instantly regretted my decision after she ran out of the ocean onto land and fell in love with a prince with her new beauty. "Why did I trade my legs away, why?" I cried to myself. Ever since my best friend escaped from the deep, dark ocean, I have been jealous of everyone and this time, I guess I have learnt my lesson. I must love myself.

Amelie Greaves (12)
Wellington School, Timperley

DRACO MALFOY: A DIFFERENT SIDE

At Hogwarts, people always say I'm the bully. But in reality, I just stand up for myself. Nobody knows the truth about me. Behind everyone's back, Harry called me and my friends muggles as we ate. When I retaliate, I get called a bully by everyone. All I want to do is enjoy my time in Slytherin and learn magic. However, Harry makes my life a living misery. He uses Hagrid to his advantage. I get picked on by him and he tricks Ron and Hermione. You see, everyone thinks I torment Harry, but it's the other way around.

George Wood (12)
Wellington School, Timperley

ROMEO

"She's dead, I knew we shouldn't have left!" I cried, yet still the tracks came. I got up and began to run, the machine tearing up the salt marsh behind me. It had been weeks since we got married and it was today, she died, torn to shreds by the approaching military drone. Whilst running, I dived behind a large rock, sheltering from the drone. We never should have moved to Marua, we thought it was nice there! But love does strange things to the mind. I still hear her cry in pain as the bullets rip her apart.

Alex Senior (13)
Wellington School, Timperley

MOTHER GOTHEL

Never have I seen such a beautiful flower. Obviously, I have heard of this flower. Why wouldn't I have heard of a flower with such great powers? I grabbed it, grasped it in my hands and sang to it. *Clop!* I ran. The queen's guards were nearby. I have never run so fast in my life. Where was I going? you ask. Only the palace, of course. They were here for the flower, for the queen, which meant one thing. The princess. I had to steal the princess. So I did.

Now, she lives in my tower. Rapunzel is mine!

Abigail Turl (14)
Wellington School, Timperley

TURNING A BLIND EYE

Barking orders at me like I was some slave, Peter rushed around trying to find Wendy as I just sat next to him, suffering. Unaware why I was feeling this pain, I fell to the floor. Peter was still oblivious. Ever since that Wendy girl came into his life, he gave her all his attention, 24/7. It wasn't fair. Why was this happening to me? In pain, just because a young boy had a crush. Weakening by the second, I tried shouting for Peter but his back was turned. I lay there looking at the ceiling, drowning in my tears.

Emma Donohue (14)
Wellington School, Timperley

HAGRID'S VISIT

On that dark, miserable night, I got on my motorbike and flew away. I was eager to meet him after all these years. I needed to deliver his letter; he had not been getting it from the mail. All I could hear in this silent night were the owls flying alongside me. But then I saw it, the small island that was home to this singular, lonely box of misery.
I flew down and parked outside in this huge storm. When I reached the house, I didn't hesitate to throw down the door, and then I said, "Harry Potter."

Nathan Collinge (13)
Wellington School, Timperley

THE BALL

As I glimpsed over, I saw an anxious-looking Cinderella running away from the ball. She slammed the doors open but suddenly, her glass slipper fell on the floor and shattered loudly. Cinderella tripped over her own foot and landed on the glass slipper. A large shard of glass was stuck in her pelvis and I saw this was my chance to make the prince fall in love with me. I ran towards him and practically threw myself at the prince. Batting my eyelashes and pouting my lips, I saw Cinderella crawling and transforming...

Rosie Brown (13)
Wellington School, Timperley

MY UGLY STEPSISTER

My dream has come true, I'm going to the ball! My hair and make-up are perfect and my dress is divine. I'm so excited! When I arrive, my mother walks Drizella and I to the dancefloor. When we catch a first look at the prince, I almost faint. But for some reason, he's got eyes on someone else - our ugly stepsister, Cinderella. What is she doing here? How dare she ruin my night. I am so upset. This is my one chance and it's been ruined by her, my cruel, evil, ugly stepsister. In a rage, I storm out.

Megan Laffly (14)
Wellington School, Timperley

MIRROR, MIRROR ON THE WALL, NO ONE SAVED HER AFTER ALL

I regret nothing. Here in this stone cell, you would think I would repent, but I won't, for I was too right in the end. I remember that very day. She was only 14 and yet the prince began to obsess over her, not that anyone noticed. I may have hated her, but nobody deserved that. The apple was a lifeline, you see, to get her out safely. She would wake unchanged and he would be gone. But he found her, kissed her, trapped her. And now she can't escape. Florian may be a prince, but not for Snow White.

Jasmine-Katie Orpet (14)
Wellington School, Timperley

HUMPTY DUMPTY

I had been stuck on the wall for hundreds of years but from the gods in heaven, a rope appeared and with no hesitation, I leapt for it. However, the weight of me was too much for the rope and it started to break. I was panicking. I didn't have the strength to jump back to the wall. It snapped and I hung on for dear life. I was hanging over a 20-foot drop. But another gift from the gods appeared. Remarkably, the king's cavalry came out of nowhere and helped me to safety. I had escaped the great wall!

George Albinson-Myers (13)
Wellington School, Timperley

THE HOBBIT: THE VICTORY OF SMAUG

I have to tell you of my victory. I woke up and I spied a pair of eyes looking at me. I ate the creature up. Breaking open the mountain, I spread out my wings and it was time for my revenge. I ate Thorin and his dwarves and burned down Lake-Town before they could fire that deadly black arrow. I set fire to Mirkwood and Rivendell, along with Hobbiton. I broke down the goblin-infested mountains and I let no one live. Every man, elf, dwarf, orc, goblin and creature was under my control. I ruled everything.

Zach Carney (13)
Wellington School, Timperley

TRUTH BEHIND THE THREE LITTLE PIGS

I was only trying to make friends. I'm sure you have all heard about the three little pigs' story that's not true. I was new in town and needed friends to find a job and home when I came across the pigs. I was the only wolf. The pigs ran away from me, so I followed them, blew their houses down and tried to speak to them. I didn't eat them! I was innocent and now I'm stuck in prison for no reason. If only they knew the real story. I get let out soon. I'm going to get revenge!

Ruby Jefferies (13)
Wellington School, Timperley

THE PREDATOR BECOMES THE PREY

Predators never win. I was forced by my pack to 'eat' this grandma. I really didn't want to, so I locked her in a closet. It was all going smoothly until the grandma's granddaughter knocked on the door. I quickly dressed like the granny and opened it. I knew that if she found out I was a wolf, I would have to kill her. As soon as she found out, I could see it in her eyes. I pounced. I was stopped by a throbbing pain in my back. The lumberjack had given me a lethal blow in the back.

Mark Taylor (13)
Wellington School, Timperley

THE BEAR THAT COULDN'T HUG

Abandoned, dishonoured, shamed! This is how I was left. But I kept my spirit. I knew that my owner wouldn't leave me for no reason. I kept at it for years, searching for my home. Finally, I found it, but I saw a new Lotso in my place. Infuriated, I stormed into Sunnyside Daycare. It was there that I learnt how to rule, raise and sadly, punish. It was there that I had to learn to survive; hiding by day, raising an empire by night. It was there that I thrived. It was there I became a grown bear.

Jenson White (12)
Wellington School, Timperley

VECNA: THE TRUTH

Nobody knew the truth about me. I didn't want anyone innocent to die. I just wanted to get revenge on the people who hurt me the most. The ones that held me captive and made me stay in that awful place. I just needed them to suffer like I did. They made me the monster I am, but too many people got involved and now they are gone all because of me. I wish that hadn't of happened, then maybe I could have had a normal life, a normal childhood, a normal family. But I hurt the people I loved.

Amelia Edwards (12)
Wellington School, Timperley

URSULA: THE TRUTH

Nobody knew the truth about me... I just wanted to be skinny. It all started when my husband, the king of the mermaids, divorced me because I was too fat. Then he made me look like I was some sort of evil witch. I was so jealous of Ariel that I cast a spell on her and made her look like me and me look like her. She was so skinny and perfect. But the curse went wrong and the king found out! He banished me to the deepest, darkest part of the sea. Why does everyone hate 'horrific' me?

Abby Cartwright (11)
Wellington School, Timperley

THE TALE OF A FISH AND A SHARK

I, Bruce, had killed Nemo. The story goes like this...
I was sleeping in my abandoned ship when a fish called Nemo swam by in a panic. While I was chasing him, he panicked me and I couldn't stop myself. It was my shark instincts. We travelled through the ship, the coral and the school whilst I continuously tried to stop myself from eating him. But on our way to do another lap, he injured his fin on some coral and that was when we both realised his life was over for definite.

Zak Clarke (12)
Wellington School, Timperley

THE NOT SO UGLY STEPSISTERS

I have to tell you the real story. You think you know about us, but it's far from the truth. We were set up by our ugly stepsister, Cinderella. The ball, our prince and her father, it's all lies. Let us tell you the truth.

It was the night of the ball and Cinderella turned. She had always been vile to us but this was worse. Shoes were being thrown, dresses ripped. I knew we wouldn't get to go to the ball but I didn't expect what Cinderella would do next...

Callie O'Neill (14)

Wellington School, Timperley

SNOW'S KILLER

Why did I do it? The sweet, innocent child, Snow, now dead. All thanks to me. The queen had a way of twisting your mind until you were enslaved to the endless misery she had put you through. Only a monster could do such terrible things. I had chased her down for days thinking I was some hero. How wrong I was. Looking into her scared and hopeless eyes. Me, holding the knife. Her skin was plump and full of life. Only a crazy man would have killed Snow.

Isla Sullivan (13)
Wellington School, Timperley

YoungWriters®
Est. 1991

YOUNG WRITERS INFORMATION

We hope you have enjoyed reading this book – and that you will continue to in the coming years.

If you're a young writer who enjoys reading and creative writing, or the parent of an enthusiastic poet or story writer, do visit our website **www.youngwriters.co.uk**. Here you will find free competitions, workshops and games, as well as recommended reads, a poetry glossary and our blog. There's lots to keep budding writers motivated to write!

If you would like to order further copies of this book, or any of our other titles, then please give us a call or order via your online account.

Young Writers
Remus House
Coltsfoot Drive
Peterborough
PE2 9BF
(01733) 890066
info@youngwriters.co.uk

Join in the conversation!
Tips, news, giveaways and much more!

 YoungWritersUK  YoungWritersCW 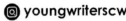 youngwriterscw